Build My Gay Dungeon

By

Bro Biggly

♂♂♂

Step into my dungeon, so-called straight guys. Step into the place where straight guys go gay.

An expert in psychological domination transforms straight guys into slobbering submissives eager to build and populate his gay party dungeon. A new sub who has never even given head is trained in every skill he needs to take a horny man from either end. A spoiled rich kid is humiliated by being ordered to join the work crew. Even a straight cop can't resist wangling an invitation. He thinks he'll get away just watching, but there are no tourists or lookyloos in this gay BDSM dungeon. Controversial themes include straight-to-gay, first-time gay encounters, and man-on-man domination/submission.

This 20,000-word gay BDSM novella includes all four complete short stories from the **Straight to Gay Leather: Build My Gay Dungeon** series, including *Find, Equip, Work*, and *Play*.

All characters are consenting adults over age 18. If you are offended by explicit descriptions of sex between men, do not read this book. All activity is safe, sane, and consenting.

♂♂♂

Copyright & Legal Note

©2018 by Bro Biggly

Models are used by permission for illustration purposes only. They are not the characters who appear in these stories.

Except for brief passages quoted for reviews and/or recommendations in magazine, radio, or blog posts, no part of this book may be reproduced in any form or by any means, electronic or mechanical, including photocopying or recording, or by information storage or retrieval system, without permission in writing from the author.

The four chapters in the Build My Gay Dungeon novella were previously published. This book contains the complete series, including:

*Straight to Gay Leather: Find (Build My Gay Dungeon #1)

*Straight to Gay Leather: Equip (Build My Gay Dungeon #2)

*Straight to Gay Leather: Work (Build My Gay Dungeon #3)

*Straight to Gay Leather: Play (Build My Gay Dungeon #4)

FIND

I looked at a lot of apartments before I found the right one. Nice place, nice neighborhood. More important, the big bear of a guy showing it around was the owner and not a droid from a rental management company. He kept checking out my ass. It's a nice ass, high and firm, and the jeans had been altered by a tailor to lift and separate my cheeks. I'm twenty-three. Dude never had a chance.

When we reached the back bedroom, I lifted my open palm like I was saying, "Stop." He did stop and looked a question at me. My answer was to use both hands to shove him back hard against the nearest landlord-white wall.

"What's your issue?" I asked. "You some kind of perv?"

He shook his head, but I pressed my hands firmly on both of his shoulders to keep him there. I'm the tall, willowy type who could have been in ballet, if ballet school wasn't for rich kids, but he was all hard muscle. Former football player would be my guess. He didn't have to let me hold him there, but he wanted me to. I'd read him right. I always do.

I put on a stern look and got right up in his face. "You've been checking out my ass the whole time. If I rent this place, is that what I have to look forward to? Some horny landlord coming around with his tongue hanging out?"

He trembled. It's cute when bears tremble. "You got the wrong idea, sir. I'm straight."

"Yeah?" I bumped my pelvis forward. He was twice as wide as me, but I was only a couple of inches shorter. When my prick bounced off his bulge, neither of us could miss the size of his old-fashioned baseball bat. "You're awful hard for a straight guy."

"That's an involuntary reflex. C'mon, man. You know how it works."

Yeah, I knew how it worked. I was reading all the signs of a big, fat hairy submissive who was in total denial about who he was. When I pushed back away from him, he groaned in spite of himself.

We both stared at the swelling in his formerly somewhat loose and sloppy jeans. Nothing loose about them now.

I folded my arms over my chest. "This is fucking ridiculous. I hope you know that."

"I'm sorry, sir."

I liked the way he kept saying, "Sir." Yeah, I could work with that.

"Take off your clothes."

"Sorry?" He swallowed hard, his big Adam's apple working up and down. I can judge age from a man's throat, and I'd say he was roughly thirty-four to thirty-seven. It's a tough age to still be in denial about your desires.

"You want me to take this place?" I gestured around the empty room.

He shrugged with his shoulder but nodded with his chin. I doubt he was aware of either motion. A classic straight guy in conflict with himself.

"I would seriously consider renting this apartment," I said, "but not if some out-of-control drooler is going to be hanging around all the time."

"I can control my drooling, sir."

"I'm not so sure you can. Consider this a test of your ability to follow orders. Take off your clothes."

See, if he wasn't a total submissive slut, he would have already told me to get the fuck out. There aren't any shortage of people looking to rent apartments in this town.

I knew what this bear wanted, if he didn't know himself.

He wanted somebody with a stronger will to tell him what to do.

Well, guess what, big guy. Today's your lucky day.

"Strip down now. I don't like to repeat myself."

He swallowed a second time, took a deep breath to gather his will, and finally grasped the hem of his cheap-shit golf shirt with both hands. My own arms remained folded sternly across my chest as I watched him slowly lift the fabric over his head. Yeah, he was a total bear. A person could go swimming in all the dark, tangled fur on his chest and belly. There was a thicker line of the fur running down from the hollow of his belly button into his jeans. The pleasure trail. A wide one.

Oh, yeah. "You don't do a lot of manscaping, do you?" I walked around him slowly to enjoy the view from every angle. He also had a hairy back, which intrigued me.

Maybe he had a hairy ass to go with? It was past time for the pants to come off.

"I don't believe in it, sir." His deep voice was stronger than I'd expected. "All that waxing. Seems kind of gay to me and, you know, I'm straight."

Yeah. Straight as a fucking ruler. I snorted. "When are the jeans coming off, big guy? Because I ain't got all day to retrain your lazy ass."

"You don't have to do this. I'm under control. I won't be drooling on you, sir."

So far, I hadn't done anything except bark out some orders. Was it my fault he was so submissive he couldn't help but obey a psychologically stronger man? "If you keep fucking off, I'm going to march right out the door and you'll never see me again."

"No, sir. Don't do that. Don't go. I'm stripping, sir. Right now. I'm cooperating, sir. Right now, you can see how fast I'm cooperating."

He toed off his shoes, unzipped his fly, started tugging and wiggling from foot to foot. How it entertains me, watching a big old bear work his way out of his clothes.

"Turn around."

He turned, the better to let me watch that wide ass emerge from the falling fabric. Yeah. Yeah. Nice and furry, just the way I like it. I unfolded my arms long enough to grab each of his muscular cheeks and yank them wide apart. There was a little knot of fur protecting his tiny beige pucker. Some fucking protection it would be from me. My prick was already dancing in my pants.

When he kicked away the jeans, he was left wearing nothing but the socks. "You can keep those on," I said. It was a small cruelty, because men feel silly wearing only socks. Especially fancy socks with little yachts printed all over them. Who bought him socks like that?

"Get on your knees, big guy."

He dropped to the thin carpet. Like all rentals, the subfloor was the cheapest possible padding. I could tell from the way he winced when he dropped.

"I like you down there. How do you like it?"

He made some mumbly sound.

"Answer me."

"I don't like it, sir."

I kicked off my own shoes and peeled off my own socks. My feet are long and pedicured, and he couldn't stop staring at the place where my flexible toes curled into the carpet. My toenail polish was shiny but see-through, and it had a way of catching the light.

"Get on all fours. Kiss my feet."

See, when I meet a potential new sub, I like to put him through his paces. Make him undergo a few tests. The foot-licking test seems minor, but you'd be amazed. A natural sub will always kiss a sexy bare foot, but a normal dude? No fucking way. Normal dudes are grossed out by feet, even the most beautiful of feet.

This bear dropped down on his belly so fast he bounced off his own swollen stiffy. His kiss was sloppy, with a lot of tongue sticking out to tease the webbing between my toes. Oh, shitfire, this dude was definitely the real fucking deal. I let him slobber and drool for a few minutes, the better to appreciate the sight of his submissive head bobbing up and down over my bare feet. My prick ached in my jeans, so I popped the fly button to give myself a little more room to expand. After that, the zipper came down by itself from the inside-out.

My toes were soon shiny from his drool, as much as from my clear nail polish. His passionate tongue squirmed into all the tender places.

"You're enjoying this a little too much," I said. "Sit back on your heels and lace your fingers together behind your neck."

He obeyed. What a luscious picture he made. His big body was completely covered with black curls, the fur thicker along his treasure trail and thickest of all at the root of his large uncut prick. I balled up my own fist and held it next to his shaft just to see. Yeah, it was what I thought. The girth of his erect shaft was larger around than my actual fist.

"Good thing you're a sub, straight guy. That thing's way too big to crawl up anybody's ass."

"I'm not a sub, sir." He managed to sound indignant. "I'm a normal straight guy. I like normal things. You're making me do this, sir."

"Mmm hmm." While my fist was that close, I might as well wrap it around that huge stalk to give it a squeeze. When I did, he spat out several sloppy pearls of pre-cum goop. "You call that normal? This is my gay hand gripping your straight prick."

"I, um, I can't help it, sir. I can't explain it, sir."

"Well, I can explain it. You pretend you want to rent this apartment so you can get young guys alone in an empty room. Then you suck their pricks. I'm not wrong, so don't tell me I'm wrong."

"But, sir..."

"What did I say?"

He hung his head, which put him in danger of getting his chin slapped by his own stiffy. Hmm. Wouldn't mind seeing that happen sometime.

"How many guys have you sucked off in this very room?" I squeezed harder, and his spithole released more drops of pre-cum.

He kept looking down, partly to avoid my eyes, but mostly because he was fixated on the sight of his big cock in my straining hand.

"Answer me," I said.

"I swear, sir. No guys, sir."

"Look at me."

He forced his head back so he could look up the long line of my lean body. It was a power position, me being clothed while he was butt-naked except for the socks, and we both knew it. My cock kept pressing at my open fly, and I knew it was only a matter of time before it popped out into the open.

"I've never sucked off any guys." His face, already pink, went red.

"You expect me to believe you've never sucked off any guys in this room."

"No, sir. Not in this room, sir. Not in any room."

Can you imagine a big old bear who sent off all these signals going thirty-five years without meeting anybody sharp enough to pick up on those signals? Holy crap.

"Well, guess what, fucker. Today is your lucky day."

"Noooooo." It was a token "no," the word he thought he should say.

Just like he thought "straight" was the label he was supposed to wear.

Despite the moans and protests, we both knew damn well he had no intention of going anywhere. There were no chains on this guy, and he was twice my size. I don't care how many martial arts classes you take. A big muscled guy is going to take down the slender muscled guy every fucking time if he really wants to.

This guy didn't want to. He didn't even want to try to pretend.

He'd waited a long time to find himself down on the ground on his knees, and he wasn't about to get up a moment sooner than he had to.

I took my time about shaking off my shoes and unrolling my socks, the better to torture him with anticipation.

He watched and waited, never making a move to get off his knees and end this game.

I liked knowing I could dominate a man just using my knowledge of psychology. It was an intoxicating form of sexual power.

"You like sucking hot pricks, don't you?" I asked, holding his eyes for a long moment.

"I don't know, sir."

"You do know. You dream about it."

"Yes, sir." His soft whisper sounded broken.

I tugged off my shirt and sent that flying too.

"Admit it. You want it, straight guy. You want this gay stiffy." I cupped my hand over the bulge in my unzipped fly.

"Yes, sir. I'm sorry, sir. I know it's pervy, sir."

I liked the broken in his voice. Fuck, yeah, I liked it a lot. His eyes bugged out as I finally— fuck, yes, finally!— grasped the top of my jeans with both hands to yank it to the floor with one smooth motion. My briefs came with, because I'm just awesome like that. A wiggle and a waggle, and my clothes were flying across the floor to smack against a far wall.

"Suck it," I said.

With his fingers still laced behind his neck, he leaned forward to inspect my personal equipment. "It's too big, sir."

"Did I ask for an opinion?" I smashed the length of my engorged shaft against his face, rubbing it hard against his cheeks and chin. He couldn't help but feel all the hot pre-fuck goo dripping out of me.

"No, sir."

"No, sir, what?"

"No, sir, you didn't ask for my opinion."

"I don't ask for any sub cocksucker's opinion. Know why? It's because I don't care what you think. I couldn't give the tiniest of tiny little fucks about what you think."

"Yes, sir. I understand that, sir."

"Then why aren't you sucking yet? You're here to do what I say, not to dilly-dally the day away."

He opened his lips to fit his face over my large, smooth, leaky peckerhead. That seemed to be as much as he could get into his mouth for the moment. Man, what a cherry. I'd been looking a long time for a bear this cherry. Which was just as well, because I'd spent a lot of time planning what I'd do once I found him. Now, grinning, I rolled my ass to demonstrate a technique I have for cupping my pelvis against a cocksucker's face. He grunted and let drool run from the corners of his mouth as he spread his lips wider and his cheeks longer.

He made a lot of noise when he sucked, the sloppy slurping noise of a guy struggling to get me balls-deep.

The struggle made it clear he wasn't a liar. I was his first, the man chosen by fate to break in this big furry beast of a bear.

"Deeper," I said. "This is fucking pathetic. Worst blow job in the world. Open your damn throat."

He made another of those gobbling, gaspy sounds and somehow stretched himself to manage another inch or so. His distended cheeks had started to develop long hollows. His throat was working up and down, and so were the long muscles inside his mouth. Because his hands remained behind his neck, his own aroused prick was completely exposed to me. It kept nudging against my knees or really anywhere he could manage to bump it while he continued to slurp down the length of my shaft.

I was thrilled, but I pretended to be dissatisfied. "Deeper," I repeated. "You heard me tell you to go deeper, boy."

A groan escaped the back of his throat, but otherwise he was muffled. I mean it, he was seriously gagged by my thrusting crankshaft. This bear was completely under my control, and all I'd really done was bark out a few trigger words.

Amazing what you can accomplish with psychological domination alone. Of course, you have to be good at spotting the subs who respond to that.

I was very, very good.

"Make me come, and I expect you to swallow, boy. Every drop that leaks out of your mouth is a stripe from my belt."

He sucked harder to pull me deeper, but sucking cock remained a challenge for him. Not too surprising since it was the very first time. He tried to keep his teeth out of play, but they brushed against my pulsing flesh from time to time. Good thing for him I didn't mind an accidental nip or two. Because he couldn't manage all of me, there were several inches of root sticking out of his face. Didn't matter. The way his throat rippled around my peckerhead was everything.

"Swallow," I said. "Swallow every drop." Even as I gave the order, I was gushing, and he was gulping. My weight, mostly on the balls of my feet up until that moment, shifted so that I was putting most of it right there on his face. He was supporting me, holding me up, using only his lips and his hard head. His mouth strained urgently around my spitting pecker, and I didn't miss the vibrations from his throat gulping hard. His Adam's apple was working overtime.

He might be new to swallowing, but he was a fucking natural because he loved it. He wanted it. That throat just kept working.

Still, because of the way his mouth was stretched open, little drops of drool couldn't help but pour out. They probably weren't my jizz, they were probably his own saliva, because of how far down I'd shot into his throat, but I pretended not to care. I wanted an excuse to punish that furry butt— a treat I wouldn't deny myself.

A single tear ran from his left eye as he finally allowed my retreating prick to escape his spread lips. Fear? Joy? Both?

"Sit back on your heels," I said.

He did, his face lifted to look up at me in perfect trust. The drool shimmered in two lines running from the corners of his mouth to his chin.

"What did I tell you?"

"To swallow."

"Did you swallow?"

"Yes, sir. I swallowed it all."

"Are you sure?" I walked over to where my jeans had landed. Picked them up long enough to unloop my belt from the denim.

"I tried, sir. I did try."

"How many drops did you spill?" An unfair question. Neither of us could know that. The mess had poured out in a stream, not in individual drops. But I enjoyed torturing him.

His eyes went wide again as he watched me double the leather belt in my right hand.

"Answer me."

"I don't know, sir. I think..." He squinted, as if looking inside himself to count something up. "Maybe... thirty?"

That was cute. This big, tough bear thought he could handle thirty strokes of my belt. Fine. Who was I to piss on his fantasy?

"Get on all fours."

At last he could drop his hands from behind his neck. He shrugged his shoulders, shook out his arms, then assumed the position. This empty room was nice in a way, although I regretted the lack of furniture, especially a mattress. The next time I stopped by, we'd have to do something about that. But I couldn't focus on "next time" right now.

This was about this time.

"Do you understand why you're being punished?" I smacked the belt against the palm of my hand to make a nasty slapping sound.

"Yes, sir."

"Tell me."

"I was sloppy, sir. I need to be trained, sir."

Ooh. For a new sub who considered himself to be straight, he did have a talent for this. "Explain. In detail. I want to hear you confess."

"I let some of your precious drops spill, sir. I was told not to do that, sir."

"Very good. How many drops did you spill?"

"Thirty, sir."

"I expect you to call out your strokes. If you don't count, they don't count. Get it?"

"Yes, sir."

How did this guy escape being captured by some horny dom way before now? He was as smoothly submissive as anyone I'd ever met.

I rubbed the doubled-up belt against his furry ass to warm it up a little. I don't care how much porn you watch or how much you fantasize about being punished, you're not prepared for the intensity of reality the first time you're actually being whipped. It's good to warm up the skin a little, to take the edge off the sharpness of the break-in blows.

He trembled beneath the belt. Anticipation can be a bitch, and he was wondering if he could really handle what was coming.

His own prick was massive, but we both ignored it. Truly a born sub, he knew better than to draw attention to himself.

Finally, I pulled back to take aim and then stroked forward. My first blow went right for the widest part of his ass, the better to connect with both cheeks at once.

"Ouch! I mean, one, sir. Thank you, sir."

A pink stripe was already forming. It made a nicely nasty contrast to the furry flesh.

I smacked him again.

"Two, sir. Thank you, sir."

A second pink stripe appeared a quarter-inch above the first. This time, I smacked him around the upper shoulders.

"The fuck? I mean, three, sir. Thank you, sir."

Ha. I liked keeping him off-balance. Some doms let new subs top from the bottom. You won't get them from me. I like to keep guys on their toes. Whip the ass, sure, but also whip some areas that sting more than thrill.

He writhed and whimpered, and I was already back to striping up the ass.

"Four, sir. Thank you, sir."

This was nice, rocking on my heels and toes to put all of my arm into each stroke.

"Seven, sir. Thank you, sir."

At fifteen I stopped and squatted so that I could rub my hands over his hot flesh. Most of the pink strokes were on his broad ass, but there was a single stripe on each of his upper thighs, as well as three on his shoulders and upper back.

"You look beautiful like that. Sweaty and submissive."

He groaned. It was humiliating to a guy like that, being told he was beautiful. Much less being told he was submissive. "Yes, sir." He had some trouble getting the words out.

I doubled up the belt again and wedged it between his buttcheeks to play it along his crack. The knot of hair over his pucker shifted, and the flesh itself bloomed open for a moment, a tiny invitation he didn't know he was offering.

"I could fuck you like this," I said. "Just like this, with you down on your hands and knees. My whole body would be rubbing into your whipped, stinging flesh."

He groaned louder.

"Say it," I ordered. "Say it in words, not in groans."

"Do it, sir," he said. "Please."

Yeah. Exactly what I thought.

"Not until this whipping is over." I stood tall again and slashed out with the belt. He hadn't expected that one so fast, and he gasped but forgot to count.

"I, uh..."

I slapped out again.

"Sixteen, sir. Seventeen, sir."

I rained down several blows much too fast for him to keep track, then stepped back. He slumped down to his belly and crawled around on the floor a little, not really trying to get away, but not able to hold himself on all fours either.

Finally, I stepped back and smacked the belt leather against my own open palm instead of his trembling backside.

"None of those count. We start again at fifteen."

He pushed himself back onto all fours.

"Tell me why."

"I'm sorry, sir. I didn't count fast enough. I lost the count."

"I told you what would happen if you lost the count."

"Yes, sir. I'm sorry. It won't happen again, sir."

Ha. He sounded sincere, but I had ways of making him break that vow. As I finished the thrashing, I considered how I was going to handle his virgin ass. I have specific cleaning rituals I require of my subs. This new guy, obviously, hadn't yet learned about that stuff. I decided I'd fuck his crack this time, instead of going inside his furry hole. He'd have to earn my prick if he wanted me deeper.

He'd have to beg for it like the sloppy, overly furry sub he was.

"Twenty-nine, sir." He gasped in pleasure/pain, the sweetest-sounding gasp in the world. His entire backside was now red and splotched from the belt, as well as shiny in random places from sweat and excitement. His fur did nothing to protect his flesh. Absolutely fuck-all nothing.

I aimed the final stroke at the exact spot where I'd aimed the first one— the widest part of his ass-cheeks. He groaned as he felt the heat renew itself there.

"Thirty, sir. Thank you, sir. Oh, fuck, sir."

He slumped back down on his belly, but he kicked his knees wide open, a silent plea for me to kneel between his thighs. His ass-cheeks were working in a way that amounted to an open confession he was grinding his hard prick into the cheap carpet. Good way to get carpet burn if you ask me, but this big bear clearly liked his pain.

"You accepted your punishment well," I said. "Better than I thought you would. I'm proud of you."

"Yes, sir."

"You have permission to tell me what you want."

"I, I..." He went suddenly shy, his face redder than his tenderized ass.

"Tell me now, or I'll withdraw the offer."

"Fuck me, sir. Fuck my ass."

"Oh, that's cute." I pretended to be shocked. "The straight guy wants his ass fucked."

"I'm just curious, sir. It's natural curiosity, sir."

Yeah, all right. I snorted, but I went back to my jeans. Dropped off the belt, fished in my pocket for supplies. Hey, you never know when you're going to meet a hottie in need of a fuck. He whimpered from his spot on the floor as he watched me rubber up.

"I don't need that." He meant the lube. Or maybe he meant both rubber and lube, who knows. "I'm straight. I've never..."

"I'm sure you're as pure as the driven snow, but I never take a guy's word for it. We'll get tested if you pass my initial trials, but for now, I'm the one in charge, so shut the fuck up."

He firmed his mouth. His ass resumed its rotating motion.

I knelt between his spread legs to squirt plenty of lube along the firm slopes of his tight cheeks, most of the small bottle going into his crack. He groaned louder and louder, mostly trying to stop himself from begging, but sometimes unable to help himself.

"Please, sir. I need, I need, I need it so bad..."

I liked sprawling on top of a big, furry guy, especially one hot and bothered from a fresh whipping. I could feel the heat of his stripes where his backside vibrated against the hot length of my naked body. My prick inserted itself boldly between his cheeks, and I began to stroke up and down. The knot of fur at his open hole tickled me, so I pressed down even more, the better to transform ticklish sensations into firm, direct pressure on my shaft.

"Inside me, sir." His voice cracked. Poor bear was about to cry.

"Not this time. You have a lot to learn about who's in control of this scene."

"Please, sir. I'm going to come. I can't help it, sir. Please, fucking please!"

"Clap your buttocks together." I smacked his right cheek, then his left.

They did clap together, although I'm not sure how much of it was under his conscious control. Didn't matter. His hard, muscular globes gripped my prick to hold on for dear life. I rocked and rotated, slipping up and down his taut, tense crack. Damn, it felt intense. This guy took direction so well it didn't matter about him being cherry. He was doing everything just about perfect.

"Harder. Clap them harder." I smacked him again.

He squirmed various muscles in his buttocks until he figured out what to do, and we settled into a hot rhythm. His buttcheeks clapped again and again on the thrusting prick trapped between them. His own prick must be experiencing untold pressure, considering the weight of our two humping bodies bearing down on top of it.

"I own you. I own this big hairy ass. I can fuck you or frustrate you. My choice. Not yours. I can whip you or please you. Always my choice."

"Yes, sir. Your choice, sir. But, please, sir, please..."

I can be merciful. Sometimes. When I'm feeling this good. "Hey, guess what. I'm going to come. You come too. Now. At the exact moment. Don't miss out."

He made a sound from the back of his throat. Probably, he was still trying to say, "Yes, sir," but he'd lost his ability to breathe.

We both blasted like bottle rockets, and he rose up a little beneath me, the better to spray his own spunk across his own belly, chest, and the cheap carpet beneath him. I settled back on my heels, tugging my prick out of his crack and yanking off the rubber at the same instant, the better to spew all my mess across the wide expanse of his stinging back.

"Yeah, you're a dirty drooler, all right." I massaged my own cream into his backside. "I knew you were a perv from the first moment I caught you checking out my ass. Admit it."

"Yes, sir," he said. "I might be a little pervy."

"I'll consider taking this apartment off your hands. But I'll expect some major upgrades."

"Yes, sir. Anything you need, sir. Anything you want. Any fucking thing at all."

EQUIP

"Boy," I said. "You know your way around a cordless drill?"

The big bear of a naked hunk sat back on his hairy haunches to stare up at me. His back, also hairy, was striped with pink courtesy several recent strokes from my belt. His lips, puffed from where he'd been sucking hard on my prick, went slack in surprise.

Boy?

He wanted to object, but he didn't have the nerve to contradict his new dom. It's cute, the way big old bears squirm when you call them, "boy." This guy was around thirty-five, but I had him under my complete control. Even though I'm only twenty-three, I'm a force of nature.

"Answer me." I'd slithered back into a pair of jeans, which was all I wore. Let the straight guy get a good look at the beautifully waxed chest of the dom who'd just whipped his hairy ass. Clutching my doubled-up leather belt in my right hand, I smacked meaningfully against my open left palm.

"Yes, sir." He swallowed, a mesmerizing motion. He had a huge Adam's apple that bobbled up and down in a way that shrieked, "Hey, man, this is a throat that knows how to suck cock and make no mistake about it."

"Yes, sir, what?" I smacked my own palm for the last time. The next time, I'd be smacking those broad shoulders.

"Yes, sir. I'm a rental investor, sir. I know my way around a hammer, nails, cordless drills, and a fucking paint bucket. Sir."

Hmm. I wasn't sure I liked his tone.

On the other hand, I much appreciated his skills.

"You'll be soundproofing this place. Walls, ceilings, floor, the whole works. I'll expect new carpet, new wall paneling, new acoustic ceiling tiles, again, everything new, the whole nine yards."

He looked around the large but empty apartment with its freshly painted walls and shampooed carpet. To obey my order, he'd have to take up the carpet and tear out the drywall.

"Don't give me the bear cub whimpers," I said. "That's five dollar a gallon cheap-shit paint and a shampoo job from the machine at the grocery store. If you expect me to live here, you're going to have to class up the place."

"Yes, sir."

"Get on your hands and knees, and come over here."

He obeyed. His buttocks were pink and red, thanks to the stripes from my belt and the pressure of sitting on his own heels. I liked watching a flushed, blotched, hairy ass wobble. He was muscular, but he still jiggled— well, at least he jiggled if I smacked him hard enough with the belt.

"Ouch! Ouch! Thank you, sir. I'm moving faster, sir. Ouch!"

I let him kneel on his haunches again. Let him lift his face to my bulging package. I shouldn't be hard again so soon after coming in his mouth and between the cheeks of his stinging ass, but I was. On a gesture from the belt, he used his deft lips to unzip my fly and work my prick back out into the open.

"Lick it. Use just the tip of your tongue. Tease me."

"Yes, sir." His breath tickled.

I could have rammed my prick straight down his throat to hammer myself to a third explosion, but I preferred to demonstrate my control. A dom who can't control himself has no business being a dom at all.

My new boy had less experience at self-control. He used the flexible tip of his oral finger to probe at my oozing spithole and then around the bulbous crown, but he was clearly itching to bring more of his tongue into play. He leaned an inch at a time into the lick job, slowly spiraling his tip around to tease me here and there, especially at the little dent. That's a sensitive area, so I curled my toes into the cheap carpet to get a grip on myself as he put more of his mouth into play.

He was a no-hands-ma cocksucker, but the fingers he'd laced together behind his neck had long ago come loose. Now his hands were held out of the way at the small of his back. With him leaning forward like that to tongue-bathe my shaft, I had a tempting view of his broad backside in all its muscular, sweaty glory.

Some temptations can't be resisted.

I smacked hard with the belt, letting it snap out of its doubled-up coil so the tongue end could slap noisily across his beautiful shoulders. "Back off."

He sat back on his haunches and looked up to show me the anguish in his eyes.

"What did I say?" I put a stern expression on my face.

"The tip, sir. To tease, sir."

"You don't have permission to bring me off again."

"I realize that, sir. I'm sorry, sir. I thought you would like it, sir."

I snorted. "You thought *you* would like it. For a straight guy, you sure like the taste of another man's spunk."

He swallowed again. His face was tomato red. All he could say was, "Yes, sir."

"In this place, you have a new name. Bear. That's your name, and I expect you to answer to it."

"Yes, sir."

"What's your name?"

"Bear, sir."

"Excellent."

His Adam's apple kept working. He was swallowing not just the last drops of my spunk, not just the last of my skin salts, but also the taste of his new name. Not too many straight guys called themselves Bear in this town. Too bad, so sad, because I was the one in charge of what he got called.

♂♂♂

One of the reasons I'd been seeking a new apartment is because I'd recently come into possession of a lifestyle sub. I wasn't entirely sure about the situation with Augur. I'd never dominated anyone twenty-four seven before, and I was concerned it would become a duty rather than a delight. Still, Augur was hard to walk away from. He was twenty-eight— a trust fund baby who had never held a job and never intended to. His life lacked direction. There was a sad story about drugs and being flunked out of several expensive colleges that never should have admitted him in the first place.

Even his family was disgusted. His father had expected him to take over the family business, but that wasn't going to happen now. All he was good for was spending money. Trouble on wheels, probably, but Bear couldn't be expected to do all the work on the new dungeon apartment by himself. He'd need an assistant, and Augur needed to learn how to work.

Hmm. A good dom doesn't just throw a couple of mismatched subs together out of nowhere. I needed to have a plan, and the plan started with Augur.

Even though I originally met him in a gay leather bar, he too was a self-proclaimed straight guy. Augur always said it was more humiliating to be dominated by a gay dude. Whatever. If Augur wanted to be humiliated, I could provide that. I could provide all kinds of that. All I knew was I figured I'd better triple-test his sincerity before the work got started.

Fine. I could do that.

Bear had one week to put together all the supplies they'd need to soundproof and re-do the apartment's interior. "Don't jack off," I said. "Not once. I want your prick well rested."

"Yes, sir."

We were too new for me to cage his equipment. Besides, I liked the idea of Bear struggling with his willpower. Struggling and, inevitably, losing the struggle. Soaping up that big dick maybe with some slippery body wash. Spewing into the shower and rinsing it away. Telling himself nobody would ever have to know. As if I couldn't read his mind like an open book.

I'd enjoy interrogating him. Punishing him. Breaking him. Watching the tears run from the corner of his eyes as he confessed...

All that was in the future. Right now, I needed to be testing Augur.

His fancy-ass condo, bought and paid for by his father, was meant to keep him on the better side of town. Away from drugs, sure, but also away from guys like me. It was a white, clean apartment, professionally decorated, with white towels and white bed linens and white curtains that were kept pristine by a professional cleaning service. He was asleep, tangled up in his white duvet and white French cotton sheets, when I used my key to let myself in.

"One o'clock in the afternoon," I said.

He blinked at the light streaming in through the open curtains. "Oh, um. I didn't know you were coming. Why you didn't you text me?"

"Get out of that bed now, Wimp."

Augur's sub name was Wimp. He hated it, but he hadn't earned anything better. Kicking out of the sheets, he immediately dropped to his knees on the plush white carpet at my feet. He spent hours training in the gym each week— why not, when he had nothing else to do?— and he'd recently touched up his golden tan at the spa. His hair too was golden, soft and buttery, utterly without red highlights. Even his brown eyes held little flecks of gold.

Everything about him was shiny, rich, and golden. Yet, on the inside, he was an empty shell that needed to be filled by somebody else's desires.

"You *are* going to learn to work, Wimp."

"Yes, sir. Are you going to pimp me out, sir?" He put his hands under his chin in a puppy dog begging gesture. He even batted his eyes.

Some straight guy. The only person he was fooling was himself.

"You'd enjoy that too much," I said. "Opening your mouth for every hairy prick with twenty dollars? Yeah, you'd totally enjoy that."

He went pink around the ears, but he didn't bother to deny it. I knew him too well.

"You're going to learn how to use a hammer. Do something useful for a change."

"But, sir!"

Wimp was clean and fresh, a tell that he'd gotten up, gone to the trouble of doing his morning business, then headed straight back to bed. Well, his lazy ass was going to be making some serious changes in the very near future.

"I don't want to hear any crap about your manicure."

"But, but!"

"Get on your belly."

He dropped onto his belly and made a kind of swimming motion to propel himself across the carpet. His wake-up prick was hard but hidden for the moment, buried in the soft fibers of the expensive snow-white carpet.

His golden thighs were lickable and whippable. Knowing what he was hoping for, I squatted between them. His golden butt-cheeks clapped open to show me the waxed, shiny crack. His pucker was pink and flexible, but he still squealed like the proverbial stuck pig when I jabbed the butt-plug into that writhing opening.

"What the— ?"

I smacked each of his cheeks in turn with my open palm. "You'll be wearing that today. Now get up and get dressed. Your clothes are in the entertainment room."

"Yes, sir." He pushed up from the floor, all his golden muscles flexing and tensing.

I followed. The plump knob of the butt-plug protruded from between his cheeks, forcing them slightly apart, enough to show the toy was securely wedged where I wanted it.

The clothes I'd bought him at the "everything's five dollars" store were stacked on the twenty-thousand-dollar Italian marble coffee table.

"Sir!"

"Put them on."

He flushed, more angry about being forced to dress in a five buck pair of gray sweatpants and a matching three dollar tee-shirt than he was about the plug in his asshole. Priorities, man. He hesitated when he picked up the package holding the buck ninety-eight dog collar. It was pink, and the silver studs were shaped like stars. More poodle than pit bull, if you get my meaning.

"I can't wear this in public. Sir. Please, sir. I'm straight. Pink, sir? A pink collar, sir? It sends the entirely wrong message about who I am."

"*I* decide what you wear. For that matter, I decide who you are."

It shamed him to buckle the pink collar around his own neck, but he wouldn't dare to disobey me. I was the man in charge here. If there's one thing I know, it's psychological domination.

"Yes, sir," he finally said.

I clipped the leash onto the collar to lead him out of his building. He'd already been trained to heel, so that part of it wasn't any trouble. He was too rich for the doorman or his fellow condo owners to make any comments about his eccentric lifestyle, although we got some side-eye in his golden elevator.

The town car and driver were charged to Wimp's credit card, but the service was one I already knew about from my connections in the gay leather community. The owners were a gay daddy/boi pair themselves, and the drivers had a relaxed attitude toward shenanigans in the backseat. Today, I actually recognized the driver as a guy I'd seen on whipping benches or hanging from chains on the wall of one of my favorite clubs. He held the silver doors open and pretended to lower his eyes, but I was left in no doubt he was keenly aware of who he'd picked up.

The driver didn't need to ask where we were going, because I'd already supplied the service with all the details. Wimp didn't need to know and knew better than to ask. We rode in silence, Wimp curling his hands under his chin in a puppy dog begging gesture from time to time. Hell, if he had to wear a pink poodle collar, he was going to play it for all he was worth. His cute ass wiggled against the seat, and I knew he was feeling the insistent pressure from the butt-plug rotating around where it counted.

He pretended to hate being a sub, but it turned him on like nothing else. Especially when he was forced to play the part of my pink-collared poodle.

It was a long drive out of the city away from the expensive condo skyscraper part of town. Wimp stared out the window as we zoomed beyond the strip malls and the hideous subdivisions where hope went to die. There was all the time in the world for me to kick back in my seat and unzip my own jeans. The sound of the zipper coming down seemed unusually loud because the driver (at my express order) hadn't put on any music.

Wimp couldn't look away from the tall, proud prick I pulled out into the open.

"You want that, straight boy?" I asked him.

"You can't walk around like that, sir. It's a health measure. I can relieve the pressure for you."

"Admit you want it."

He glanced nervously toward the front seat, but the driver was a professional and gave not the slightest sign he was aware of what we were doing. Pre-cum was already streaming down my tall shaft.

"Yes, sir," he said. "Please. I want it. Let me taste it. I need to know what it tastes like."

Tastes the same as it did the last time you sucked me off.

But I repressed the urge to mock him. The cheap-shit clothes, the collar, the third person in the sedan, the being required to beg for what he needed... that was enough to meet all his humiliation needs.

"Take it," I said. "But do a good job. An expert job. I want some evidence you're learning how to do this thing. I expect you to swallow every drop."

"Yes, sir. I'll make you proud, sir. I'll lick it good and clean."

"You'd better."

He squirmed around to get his face in my lap. At that precise instant, the driver turned left, and Wimp's face was smacked harder by my prick than he'd expected. Little specks of pre-cum slapped across his cheeks, and his mouth opened wide to deepthroat me without much of anything in the way of warm-up. It was a far cry from the first time he'd tentatively swiped his tongue across my crown. Back then, all flushed and cherry, he'd even wept a little, telling me it was way too big for his mouth. A lie, of course. He was a natural intended by fate to serve as a semi-pro cocksucker.

Now, after weeks of training, his flexible, spreadable mouth opened as if he'd been born to fit his face over my throbbing erection. His throat worked, and I knew he was consciously gulping his Adam's apple up and down, the better to send some extra vibrations into my shaft.

His tongue and his throat were talented, no doubt about it. However, at the moment, it was those stretchable lips that were putting most of the pressure on my crucial places.

I still held the leash, and I tugged it a little, enjoying how it felt when I pulled on his neck. Enjoying the desperate way he clamped down. The way he twisted to make sure I wouldn't fall out of his impetuous mouth.

"You're a cocksucking wimp, Wimp." I said it oh-so-softly, the better not to be overheard by the driver, although I didn't really much care either way.

Wimp gurgled around the fat flesh wedged so far down his throat.

"You're getting off on this. Your sweatpants are bunched up in front from your pathetic hard-on."

He squirmed some more. Drool was running from the places where my shaft held his mouth open.

"Come in your pants like the nasty wimp you are." It was a cruel order because I knew he couldn't. Not yet. The butt plug had him on the edge, as did the taste of my male juices, but he needed something gripped around his cock.

There was nothing to slow me down, though. I chuckled and then thrust. Wham. There I was, emptying my load in the back of his struggling throat.

The driver turned again, this time into a gravel parking lot outside a large barn. Perfect timing.

Wimp tucked me back into my pants. There was agony in his eyes and a large tent pitched in his sweatpants. Too bad, so sad, so not my problem.

We had arrived at our destination.

The driver, as instructed, stayed in the town car. I jerked on Wimp's leash.

"Let's go."

A man almost as big and hairy as Bear himself waited inside. The so-called cabinetmaker, although he made a lot more than cabinets. The rest of the staff was nowhere in sight. All in accordance with what I'd pre-arranged.

"Right on time, sir. Good to see you."

I didn't need the chitchat. "Show me."

He nodded and walked toward an ebony bedframe with multiple spotlights turned to illuminate the project. Wimp's father's credit card had also paid for this, although it was coded as, "Fine Art." There were no box springs or mattress on this wooden frame, just the frame itself complete with four stout posts intricately carved in a style he'd copied from German Renaissance masters. Of course, the German masters turned their attention to much different subject matter. Perhaps souls writhing in hell, or some such. Whereas Cabinet had carved endless, interlocked images of big-thighed and big-cocked men fucking, sucking, and grinding.

Wimp whimpered.

Erotic art wasn't what shocked a man of his class. What shocked him were the number of D-rings set in place in the stout posts.

Heavy blue steel chain hung from each of those D-rings.

"We'll need to test the structural integrity," I said.

STRAIGHT TO GAY LEATHER: BUILD MY GAY DUNGEON

Cabinet nodded. "Of course, sir. Should I give you privacy?"

I snorted. "No, I'd like you to observe. You may get undressed and kneel."

Wimp whined louder.

Cabinet, an experienced switch who rarely got to play the sub anymore, wasted no time in losing his clothes. There was already a black leather pillow on the floor near the bed, which told me he'd anticipated my wishes. Good. I liked that about Cabinet. He knew what he wanted, and he knew what I wanted too.

"I can't," Wimp said. "While he's watching?"

"You are not the one in charge here," I said. "I'm in charge."

"Yes, sir. I understand I need direction, sir."

Cabinet had a very large prick with a beer can circumference. Wimp tried not to look at it, but he couldn't help stealing little glances that way.

"Are you afraid?" I asked.

He swallowed.

"Speak. Don't make me whip you in front of my friend."

"Yes, sir. A little. It's too big, sir."

"You need to be afraid. Fear is something that's been missing in your life. Fear motivates. Do you understand me?" When I dropped his leash, it made a loud clatter on the hard floor. "Strip off everything but the collar."

"Yes, sir."

Cabinet's eyes glittered with appreciation as Wimp's golden body came into view. The pampered skin, the ridged muscle.

The oblong handle of the plug wedged into his hole.

"Stand," I said.

He obeyed, and I spread his curvy butt-cheeks far apart, the better to show off the plug.

"Back up against my friend."

Wimp backed up, while Cabinet lifted his face to meet him. A man of Cabinet's experience had no trouble grasping the plug's handle between his teeth to pull it free of the sucking hole. Wimp gasped as he felt the device pop free, but he dared not beg or protest. His hands, loose at his sides, balled into fists.

"Turn around."

He turned, and his hard prick slapped against Cabinet's face. Cabinet thrust out his tongue to wipe up the long streamer of pre-cum, but he knew better than to suck without my express permission.

"Spread-eagle yourself on your belly on the frame. We're going to test the equipment and see if it's good enough to earn its spot in my dungeon."

I'd let go of his leash, and it dragged along the floor, making a noise that sounded like Wimp's submission. The wooden slats on the mattress-free frame couldn't be all that comfortable against his naked body, but they'd support him well enough, and that's all that mattered. He found a way to spread-eagle himself so I could easily secure the chains around each of his wrists and ankles to hold his four limbs to the four bedposts. His prick pointed hard and out between the slats, so he'd splash all over the floor if he came. His butt-cheeks were still gapped open to expose the pink, flushed pucker so recently filled by my plug.

"Yes, I'm going to test these posts. I'm going to test them hard."

He whimpered and closed his eyes, probably expecting me to use one of the many whips displayed from a rack on a nearby wall. We had two hours, so I could give him some of that, but pain was for him, not for me. And, right now, my balls were starting to scream.

Time to open my fly again. Wimp and I had already made the clinic visit to exchange our health tests, so I didn't need any rubber. Just the lube. An expensive jar also charged to Wimp's daddy's credit card. Something from France that smelled of rich college boy's privates.

"Look at that winking asshole," I said. "He loves being fucked up the butt."

"I can see that, sir," Cabinet said.

"I'm straight." Wimp tried to sound indignant, but he must have failed his theater class too. "This is totally happening under protest."

"This will be a painful fuck," I told him. "A jackhammer. It's the only way to test the structural integrity of this piece."

If anything, his pucker bloomed even wider. I crooked three fingers inside of him and scissored around to make sure the lube was getting in everywhere. His pain entertained me, but I intended to enjoy a smooth ride for myself. Each time I pressed on his gland, he rattled his chains.

"Please," he said. It broke him, being forced to beg for an assfuck. That's why I did it. "Please, sir. Please. I need your jackhammer. I need it deep."

"Crawl under the bed," I said to Cabinet. "If this thing collapses, it's falling on you because it was your work."

He grinned. "It won't collapse, sir." Wriggling under the bed, he positioned himself so he could swallow Wimp's prick at the exact instant I gave the order.

That was the sandwich. Wimp chained belly-down on the bedframe, his prick protruding through the slats to fill Cabinet's mouth. Me sprawled on top of Wimp, my drooling, dripping prick shouldering its way between his muscular cheeks. His pucker surrendered without a fight, opening wide from my first thrust.

"Please, sir," he said. "Harder. Harder."

I'm going to hold you to that...

Cabinet made those happy, gobbling sounds of a man sucking a prick that's the perfect size to fill his mouth. Each time I slambanged into Wimp's throbbing ass, I knew I was sending a jolt into Cabinet's mouth too. From time to time, I glanced at the D-rings set into the wooden posts, because those joins were the most likely point of weakness, but they held like they'd somehow merged to become a single organic piece.

The clips that locked the chains in circles around Wimp's wrists and ankles dug into his flesh, creating bright red imprints in his golden skin. It had to hurt, but the way his guts kept clamping hard on my thrusting prick told me how much he welcomed the hurt.

"Don't come," I said. "Neither of you is allowed to come."

Unfair, of course. I knew they couldn't obey. Their bodies would override their will. Grunting, slamming, I took care to hit Wimp's prostate in all the right spots. A direct assault on his willpower, which resulted in an indirect assault on Cabinet's.

The feel of me spurting inside of Wimp, the smell of me spurting...

Too much.

No man could resist that trigger.

They came together, Wimp shooting neatly and deeply into Cabinet's throat, but poor Cabinet spewing helplessly over his own body and the underside of the bedframe.

It took five minutes or so for me to empty my nuts. The aftergasms lit up the insides of my thighs, and it would be easy to slump on top of Wimp. Easy to sleep. For a minute, I even pretended that was what I'd do, and I could feel the both of them relax beneath me.

Fuck that.

With a sudden roar, I was on my feet to snatch the single-tail off the wall display.

"You both disobeyed, and you will both be subject to the whip while I continue to test this bedframe."

Wimp first, of course, since he was already chained in place. Cabinet had to kneel again on the leather pillow, his belly and chest smeared with his own goop, as he watched me slam again and again across Wimp's exposed backside. I hit hard enough to make those four bedposts walk across the floor. Despite the stoutness of their construction, they couldn't help moving a little, but they were sound and would never, ever break. This evil bed of torture was pure genius, hell, Cabinet himself was genius for putting it together.

The money Wimp's father had paid for this so-called, "Fine Art" couldn't have gone into a better project.

Wimp shrieked shamelessly under the whip. Nobody's stoic beneath the single-tail. His back, ass, and thighs were an intricate pattern of red, raised stripes. Pain slut that he was, he seemed to shriek as much in triumph as in agony.

He was getting what he needed. What he wanted.

His prick, already hard again, protruded from the wooden slats.

Cabinet, waiting, had also developed a renewed stiffy.

Everywhere I looked, I saw wood. We didn't really need any further tests, but I saw no harm in devoting another two or three hours into making sure everything and everybody were as durable as I wanted. After all, if this item was going to become a permanent fixture in my dungeon, I wanted to be one hundred percent certain it could stand up to the job.

WORK

Bear met Wimp for the first time in the service parking lot behind Bear's building. It was three in the morning. No moon, no stars, just the smudgy gray-black of a cloudy night poorly lit by a single orange streetlamp. They were both wearing denim, work boots, and flannel shirts, but Wimp's shirt was unbuttoned several buttons, the better to show off his pink poodle collar and his shiny waxed chest.

"Who the hell?" Bear asked. "Or should I say, what the hell?"

"Meet your crew," I said. "You need a second pair of hands to install my dungeon."

"That guy is..."

I folded my arms over my chest and looked stern. "What did you think I had planned when I asked you to pass a health test?"

Bear swallowed. Sex is what he'd thought. Rubber-free sex. But he hated to admit it, because he was still invested in his self-image of being straight. "Look, I came here to work, that's all."

"Wimp has passed his health test too. But that isn't the only test I expect you boys to pass. You have to serve as useful slaves, or I won't keep you in my stable."

Bear folded his own arms over his chest, a disobedient posture which couldn't be tolerated. "That guy is not a worker. No way he's a worker. He came to play." Because of his sheer size and bulging muscles, Bear was used to intimidating other men, but he should know by now that he couldn't intimidate me.

"Get on your knees." My stern voice promised immediate consequences if he dared to disobey.

Suddenly nervous, Bear looked around the parking lot. It was still three in the morning, and we still had the place to ourselves, yet he felt painfully exposed. Wimp and I could read Bear's emotions in the reluctant way he knelt within the beam of the orange streetlamp— a light which seemed much brighter than it had only moments before.

"Wimp, step forward," I said.

Smirking and preening, Wimp obeyed, his hips swaying with a sassy little wiggle-waggle.

Uh oh, I had not one but two cases of attitude on my hands this fine morning.

"Take off your jeans."

Wimp kept shaking his ass. "I can just open my fly."

Yeah, that was some attitude, all right. Moving slowly to underline my actions and my authority, I unlooped the belt from my own jeans. "Don't make me repeat myself."

"No, sir." Wimp gulped, knowing he'd pushed me a tad too far.

His ass shimmied around as he bent and squatted to remove his boots. I tolerated the way he was showing off since he needed to be barefoot to unpeel the tight denim. Bear, kneeling, looked even more nervous than before, but he knew better than to whine about the potential for exposure. Besides, Wimp had excellent legs— long and lean, with well-defined thigh muscles that pointed directly to Wimp's proud package. Bear liked watching them come into view.

We both did. It was a lickable sight.

Bear leaned forward on his knees. "Hey, the dude waxes his balls?"

I smacked my doubled-up belt against his shoulders. "Did I ask for your opinion?"

"No, sir."

"Since you're so fascinated with Wimp's balls, take a closer look. Lean forward a little more. Yeah, that's it. Stick your tongue out. All the way out."

This was an order Bear was happy to obey. His muscular back strained attractively beneath his flannel shirt as he thrust his tongue into Wimp's taint, the better to explore the sweep of shiny flesh from his pucker to the base of his stalk. Waxed skin, especially in the most personal places, holds a special fascination for furry men like my Bear.

I could be merciful. "You have permission to suck him inside your mouth."

Groaning as he squeezed his eyes tightly closed, Bear stretched his mouth wide open. He was the classic case of a guy being able to resist anything but temptation. His lips folded themselves over Wimp's smooth head, and Wimp stepped back a half-step, the better to tease. Of course, Bear leaned even further forward to swallow more.

"You have permission to suck him as deep as you want to. Balls-deep if you want to."

Bear hated that, being given the option. He'd like it better if I insisted. That way, he could kid himself about what he wanted. He could tell himself he was really straight. That he was deepthroating this guy to please me, because I was holding the belt and giving the orders.

Tough. The best kind of domination involves getting into the sub's head, and I no longer wanted him to be able to kid himself. This was one big old hairy bear of a man-mountain who needed to figure out he wasn't as straight as he claimed.

"Oh, that's good. I like your enthusiasm. You're enjoying this. All the best cocksuckers enjoy their work." I chose the words carefully, to taunt him as well as to instruct him. "That's soooo good. All the way. Yeah. I like to see your throat like that."

His Adam's apple worked up and down. Wimp was rather passive at first, just standing there naked with his feet braced apart on the asphalt surface, the better to hold himself still to accept Bear's suction. He didn't want to give anything. He just wanted to accept. My own prick shifted in my jeans, although I didn't yet unzip my fly.

As the dom, I wasn't about to let my happy ass go hanging out in public parking lots. That crap was for subs.

As he surrendered to Bear's oral skills, Wimp's eyes crinkled shut with pleasure, and his hands shaped themselves into two tight fists. He wanted to grab onto Bear's face and pull it all the way down his shaft, but he was still forcing himself to hold back.

To accept. To receive.

But not to give. Because he was determined not to give. Determined not to thrust. Fine. It must be a point of pride with Wimp, not to give to another sub. I could see all the psychology at work here. That was my job, getting into their heads.

So Bear worked his mouth up and down Wimp's long, hard pole. Despite the orange glare of the streetlamp, his face had shadows from the forceful way his suck job hollowed out his cheeks. Slobber was already running down his chin.

STRAIGHT TO GAY LEATHER: BUILD MY GAY DUNGEON

I smacked his shoulders with the belt again. A harder snap, but it wouldn't feel like pain this time. Instead, it would feel like a spur.

Gulping hard, clearly excited, Bear somehow found a way to choke down not just Wimp's entire shaft but his waxed balls too. How did he get so much raw meat in his mouth, if he was a nearly cherry straight guy? That crap takes practice. His jaws must ache from his efforts. The strain in his face, shoulders, and neck looked painful in a sexy way that can only lead to ecstasy.

Wimp, trembling, blinked his eyes open again to look at me over Bear's bobbing head. He moaned softly but didn't try to form words. He probably knew he couldn't make a sensible request.

Didn't matter. I knew what he wanted. I knew everything inside of him. An intuitive dom, I could see right through him.

"Yes," I said. "You have permission. Come. Come hard. Spray it all the way down his throat."

♂♂♂

Three hours later. All the construction materials were inside the building, although some of them remained stacked in the lobby or in the hall. Bear and Wimp worked fast, though, and they'd already completely installed the soundproofing on the ceiling, walls, and even the floor of my apartment. To test the quality of the materials, I decided to make them shriek.

After all, if you've got a dungeon in an apartment building, you better have quality soundproofing.

"Bear," I said. "Naked and on your back."

"Yes, sir." We were in the living room, which was spacious, especially without furniture, but his big hairy body still seemed to take up a shocking amount of surface area.

"You get naked too," I said to Wimp. "Everything but the collar."

"Yes, sir."

I tossed a tube of lube toward Wimp, who caught it one-handed while kicking off his jeans.

"Sit on his prick."

"Yes, sir."

Wimp squatted over Bear, his long feet planted on either side of Bear's ears, the better to glop lube all over Bear's prick while giving him a close-up view of his waxed, shiny pucker. Then he fingered himself with more glops of the lube.

Bear moaned. "I hope you don't think that's turning me on. I'm straight, dude."

"That makes two of us."

"Two of us what?"

"We're both straight. We're only doing this because..." Wimp gestured at me. "He has some kind of hold on us somehow."

I smirked. Psychological domination, that's what I do. Sure, I can whip and shackle a sub, but there are plenty of bigger guys than me out there. It's my mind that allows me to twist so-called straight guys into whimpering, simpering, cock-hungry submissives.

"Stop nattering, and sit on his prick, or you both get an ass-whipping," I said.

"Yes, sir." Wimp pulled two shiny fingers out of his own pucker with an audible pop that drew attention to how dilated and ready he was. My prick stirred in my jeans as I watched him scramble around to get into the right position— face-to-face, Wimp on top, his curvy bubble-butt adjusting its angle so he could lower himself slowly on Bear's hard shaft.

A mouth-watering view, if I do say so myself. My two slaves looked beautiful together.

After some wriggling, Wimp's hole notched onto Bear's prickhead. Boom. He sat down hard, then lay down long while keeping his asshole wrapped around Bear's shaft, a Wimp-on-top fuck position that trapped his own shaft between their writhing bellies. Definitely delicious. I walked around to study the two of them slow-fucking from every angle.

At that less-than-ideal moment, someone rapped hard on the closed but not locked door. It just isn't practical to lock up when you're doing construction, is it?

If I ignored the knock, they might let themselves in.

Wimp and Bear, still interlocked, went still as an obscene marble statue.

"Don't stop," I said, my voice calm but stern.

Wimp buried his face in Bear's furry chest, but he renewed the efforts to work his smooth ass around Bear's prick. Guy at the door or no guy at the door, they couldn't have unknotted themselves if they tried. They were too turned on.

Another series of raps sounded.

"All right, all right." I went to the front door and checked the peephole. It was what and who I thought, the super. He was a big, burly black guy, with lots of muscle, good cheekbones, and an exasperated expression on his face.

Sure wouldn't mind getting a taste of that. I opened the door a crack.

"How long are these construction materials going to be in my hallways?" he asked. "There are fire codes."

"We're going to install the floor today, and then we can move the rest of the materials into the apartment out of the way. There won't be anything left in your hallway after five o'clock this evening." I studied his handsome face to judge his reaction. "The whole project will be done in three days tops."

"Mmm-hmm." He looked skeptical.

"Three days, maybe even two days if my crew works fast enough. Then you can inspect the improvements for yourself. I think you'll be pleased."

"What's the sound?"

"What sound?" I batted my eyelashes.

"Somebody screaming like a catamount in heat."

This wasn't a failure of the soundproofing. He could hear that stuff out in the hall because I had the door open. (By the way, I didn't know what a catamount was, either. Later, I looked it up on my phone. Spoiler alert. It's a mountain lion.)

"Screaming?" I batted my lashes more emphatically.

The super pushed his way past me. Only because I let him. I was playing the part of the pushover, the better to lure this sexy beast into my lair.

"Holy fuck." He folded his arms over his chest and stared, open-mouthed, at the two naked guys going at it all over the newly installed subflooring. Maybe he thought Wimp's pink poodle collar clashed with the bright blue of the soundproofing material. Or maybe he couldn't believe how much spunk he was spewing all over Bear's furry body. "Three days tops, huh? Because this sure the fuck doesn't look like your crew puts a high value on getting the job done."

"They were on their break." I snapped my fingers. "And now the break's over. Get dressed, boys. Mr..." I looked at the super.

"Stevens," he said.

"Mr. Stevens needs you to get the floor installed so we can move the rest of those boxes out of the halls."

"Yes, sir." Bear squirmed out from underneath Wimp, not even bothering to wipe himself off before he pulled his jeans back on. Didn't bother me. Spunk is a good body lotion, right? High in protein and all that.

Wimp, almost cross-eyed from the force of the spew he'd emptied all over Bear's chest, felt around for his own clothes for a minute or two. I finally took mercy on him and kicked them in his direction.

Two straight guys wouldn't normally be so relaxed about being caught fucking by a stranger, but they were too dazed from the afterglow to give the super much thought.

Let him stare. Let him get an eyeful.

"You'll find I'm better at motivating my workers than most bosses," I said.

Stevens kept shaking his head. "This is not how I've ever seen any construction crew operate." His straight-guy trousers were cut generously to accommodate his package, but they seemed to be thickening up in the appropriate space.

I kept my chill. "The job *will* be completed on time, probably ahead of time, or I'll know the reason why."

"I'll bet." He eyed my jeans, which were tented in front and even a little spotted from some pre-cum leakage.

For the first time, I acknowledged that I knew where he was gawking. "Want a taste?"

"I, um, no. No offense, but I'm straight."

Yes, it was pretty much what I'd already figured. Another straight guy. I must be a magnet for these dudes.

"No offense taken," I said. "Only, if you want us to get this work done, I guess you better clear out for now."

"I, um, I could help you with this flooring. The sooner those boxes are out of my hallways, you understand..."

"Sure. I understand. Fire codes."

As if. This so-called straight guy couldn't walk away. Fine by me, because I had no intention of letting his muscular ass walk away.

As the saying goes, I love hard work, and I could watch it all day long. Wimp wasn't as good or as big as the other two, but he had a cute wiggle in his ass when he worked. They were all three of them super-enthusiastic about getting the job done. I drifted around, a bottle of sparkling water in my hand, as I examined their straining, sweaty muscles from every angle. As long as they kept going back and forth with boxes, they had to keep their clothes on, because it was full daylight now, and people were coming or going from the other units. A couple of Bear's nearest neighbors looked in to see what he was doing.

"Oh, that's a good idea, soundproofing," one of the guys said. "I wish I could afford to have that done."

Bear shrugged. "It isn't as expensive as you think. And it will be well worth the money."

"Hmmm."

With three guys down on their hands and knees, the laminate flooring went down fast. By lunchtime, the last of the boxes had been stacked up in what would be a normal human's dining room. The walls and ceiling were still uncovered blue soundproofing material, but it was time for another break. Stevens was still hanging around, obviously reluctant to leave. For a straight guy into obeying the fire codes, he seemed awfully eager to see what me, Bear, and Wimp would do next.

"We're heading off to lunch," I said.

"Hey, tell you what." Stevens hesitated. He was having trouble getting the words out. Poor bashful baby.

"All right. What?"

"I'll buy the lunch if you guys talk to me a little more about..."

"About what?" I lifted an eyebrow.

He blinked and looked down at his feet. "You know what. Your unusual methods of motivation. I'm thinking of renovating some places myself, and I'm open to learning."

I'll bet you're open to learning. Way, way open.

♂♂♂

Stevens took us to a little Vietnamese place with the kind of booths that have curtains on them. It was a place I'd heard about where crime guys had lunch, and maybe they did, but I saw a glimpse of blue in one of the booths, so I knew police ate there too. Basically, it was a place where you could eat and talk in semi-privacy, instead of having everybody else in town involved in your conversation, the way it was at so many other over-crowded lunch places.

The waiter dropped off our beer and pho, then drew the curtain. It was me and Bear on one side of the booth, Wimp and Stevens on the other. Stevens kept shooting side-eye at the pink dog collar.

"On your knees, Wimp," I said.

"Yes, sir." Smirking, Wimp slithered in a slinky slide down underneath the table. Stevens automatically spread his knees, although I'm not sure if he was consciously aware of the message he was sending.

"Unzip his zipper."

Wimp used both fingers and lips to open Stevens's fly. The tabletop obscured some of the scenery, but Bear and I had the general idea. Stevens's prick was roughly the size and color of a summer eggplant, the kind left on the vine too long to get too big. Wimp smacked his lips but he knew better than to start licking and kissing all over it without my express permission.

Stevens groaned softly, an involuntary sound from the back of his throat. "I'm not gay, man, I'm not, I'm really not."

"Nobody's saying you're gay," I said. "This is about human physiology. About getting things done. Men are motivated by male hormones, especially testosterone, and nothing stimulates testosterone so much as being around other high testosterone males. It's the competitive instinct."

"That makes sense." Stevens shifted on his ass-cheeks, a way to poke his fat prick at Wimp's face. "I mean, I'm not turned on by dudes, man, so there had to be a reason why my dick is so hard."

"You need to clear the pipes," I said. "You'll work better this afternoon if your blood pressure isn't so high, know what I mean?"

"Mmm. Not sure that I do. Maybe a demonstration?"

"Suck him off, Wimp." I finally gave the order we'd all been waiting for, and Wimp clamped his flexible lips over Stevens's crown.

That tight mouth of his looked gorgeous with Steven's flushed-purple pole sticking out of it.

Stevens himself went cross-eyed. "Wait, man. Right here? In the restaurant?"

As if he hadn't taken us to this place for a reason. Laughing, I tugged harder on the curtain to make sure it was completely closed. Also, to underline the fact Stevens had taken us to the kind of restaurant that has curtains on the booth.

Accepting my unspoken challenge, Stevens closed his eyes, the better to focus on the sensations coming from the gifted mouth gliding up and down his swollen shaft. I had no idea if he'd had any previous experience with men. If he had, he'd know Wimp was an exceptionally well-trained cocksucker.

Even if he hadn't, he'd know Wimp was a rare talent.

"He has no gag reflex at all," I said. "You can feed him everything."

Wimp, determined to prove I was no liar, stretched his entire face over the length of that swollen purple cock. Bear and I could no longer see even so much as an inch of shaft. All we saw was the bobble-dance of Wimp's bouncing head.

Because of his size, Bear couldn't get under the table and copy Wimp's moves. However, I took mercy on him and moved his huge hand down to my package. "Take it out," I said. "Play with it any way you want."

"Yes, sir!" He wasted no time in getting me out into the open. His big hands squeezed my shaft, while his tongue stroked forward to lick at the oozing spithole. A strangled cry told me Stevens was shooting down Wimp's throat, which triggered my own eruption. Bear's lips formed a wide O to catch the spiral of my spraying drops. Some of the mess escaped to slap the side of his mouth, but he captured most of it right away. His Adam's apple bobbed as fast as Wimp's head. Up and down. Down and up.

So nasty. As I relaxed, I heard the mutters outside of the boys in blue paying their check and getting ready to leave the restaurant.

They had no idea of what we'd gotten away only a booth away.

I felt satisfied, not just physically but mentally.

Remembering we were actually here to eat lunch, we settled back into place and picked up our forks. Stevens seemed dazed by what he'd just done, while Wimp seemed a little smug. He was proud of the effect his mouth had on so-called straight guys. Still, we were just four respectable diners finishing up our pho by the time the waiter opened the curtain to drop off the check.

"A public place, man," Stevens finally said. "With cops in the next booth."

"Behind a curtain," I said. "And they were behind their own curtain too. Anyway, what's done is done. Now it's back to work."

♂♂♂

My three straight guys did what straight guys do best—manual labor. It was hot in the condo, and they'd all taken off their shirts, the better to expose acres of straining muscle. Bear's furry torso was in striking contrast to the smooth chests of Wimp and Stevens.

Wimp, I knew, got a professional wax job, but Stevens's smooth muscle was all-natural. At the moment, he was on a short stepladder that allowed him to install acoustic ceiling tiles over the blue soundproofing. Already tall, he looked like a giant with his bulky, bulging arms lifted overhead.

He needed a sub name. I refused to use real-world names in my dungeon.

My cock stirred, but I didn't want to distract them from their work when they were making so much progress. Those famous fire codes, you know. "I'm heading out for forty-five minutes. I expect you boys to have this job finished by then, or I'll be whipping some ass."

"Yes, sir." The three of them practically sang it out in a chorus. Even Stevens knew the right answer.

Out the door and into the street. I walked maybe half a block away before I ran into a tall, uniformed police officer. "Scott," I said. "Thought I saw you behind one of those curtains at the restaurant."

"Maybe you did, and maybe you didn't, but I for sure saw you. Up to your old tricks again?"

I made an elaborate shrug with my shoulders that somehow ended up with my chin pointing in the direction of a nearby park with a lot of friendly hedges. Scott was an ex, so he had no trouble reading my body language. We walked over there, while he continued to talk my ear off about the same issues he'd always yapped about.

"Perverting straight guys might be legal, but we both know it should be a crime."

"You loved it when I perverted you." I guided him around to a forgotten concrete bench hidden in a secret circle of overgrown hedges. The lack of trash told me nobody had found this spot since the last time Scott and I used it ourselves.

"Sit," I said. "Sit, Cop."

He was no longer Scott, my ex. He was a horny, desperate Cop who didn't get what he needed from the blondes he met on hookup apps. Groaning, he sat immediately, because my tone of voice assured him I wasn't interested in a runaround.

"Open your fly."

He unbuttoned and unzipped to allow his proud spike to grow tall in the open air. There's something about a big fat man-spike sticking out of a pair of black uniform trousers, especially when professional items like handcuffs, flashlight, and firearm are shifting around on a heavy police belt.

"Look how big you are. Some straight guy. I bet you can lean over and suck your own cock."

He whimpered.

"Do it, Cop. Suck your own cock."

He tried. His back arched, and his head bobbed down, but he simply wasn't that flexible, especially not wearing his full uniform. Of course, I'd known that. I'd wanted some reason to torture him.

Without further ado, I snapped the handcuffs off his belt and used them to lock his hands out of the way behind his back. Then I slowly, teasingly began to use my own mouth to dribble drool up and down the length of his stalk.

"No, not here. Please. What if somebody sees?"

His shiny glans was plump and almost the same size as my balled-up fist. I sucked it into my mouth and spun it around.

"Noooooo."

I rocked back on my heels, spitting him out. Of course, his prick-head went flying up, which caused a string of pre-cum drops to spray forward. Luckily for him, the drops didn't smack into my chin, but instead fell a little short and down to the ground.

He looked down at me, agony in his eyes.

Smirking, I said, "I guess I'll be going then. Since you said no. Since you're so, so worried about being seen." But I made no move to get back on my feet.

"You live to torture me, Bryan, don't you? You honestly do."

I fluttered my eyelashes at him. "What do you call me?"

He groaned. "Sir. You live to torture me. Sir."

He was going in the right direction, but I needed more, so I fluttered my lashes again. "I have no idea what you could possibly mean."

"You have to make me beg, don't you?"

"You need to convince me you want it. I have a lot of subs demanding my time. I can't devote my attention to the unwilling and the uncertain."

"Fuck you." He started to get up, and all that crap hanging off his police belt rattled around, but I noticed his prick wasn't going soft. "Unlock my hands."

Pushing myself off the ground, I waggled the silver key in front of his eyes. "If I unlock those cuffs, you're not getting fucked today. Your choice, your decision. But don't think you can go back and change your mind."

He backed his thighs against the bench again and sat down hard. There was no more discussion about unlocking the stainless steel cuffs. Instead, he walked his buttocks up and down where he sat, the better to shake his erect flesh in my direction. More pre-cum was running down his shaft. Cop had always been a juicy fuck. No real need for lube with this guy, although I always used a rubber, since we weren't a regular thing and I had no idea if he was fucking somebody else or who it was.

It had been a while since he'd experienced my talent for sliding on a rubber using only my mouth. Groaning, he poked his prick several inches down my shaft as I worked.

"Sooo good," he moaned. "Dear fuck, how can it feel like this? It's so wrong. I didn't come from this kind of background."

I couldn't answer. I was too busy tease-licking him through the rubber. It wasn't nearly enough intensity for either of us.

He moaned louder. "All right, all right. Don't make me beg. Don't break me. Please, Bry... I mean, please, sir. I need it so bad. You know how bad I need it. You're making me feel this way somehow with that evil tongue of yours."

I loved breaking him, not just because he was a cop and not just because he was an ex, but because he kept insisting he was straight. For the second time in ten minutes, I spat him out, although carefully, so I could be confident the rubber stayed in place. Standing, I slowly— oh so slowly— began to shimmy-shake out of my jeans. There was no way to do what I needed to do without kicking off my shoes so I could work my pants completely off. It was a process that took time, know what I mean?

"Please. I hate saying please. But please." Cop was practically crying.

Then I was naked, then I was on him just that fast. I must have devoted ten seconds or so to dabbing some lube on my own pucker, but I don't remember that part. The important thing was how I ended up. My legs wrapped tightly around his waist, so I couldn't avoid feeling his steel-cuffed wrists behind his back. My arms clutched like bands around his shoulders. My long, slurping hole stretched out tight over his upthrust prick. Rocking in his lap, I controlled the pace of the fuck. When I leaned back, I could look into his eyes, although he wasn't really looking back at me, because they were completely blank from the intensity of what he was feeling.

Certain interior muscles began to pulsate up and down the length of his shaft.

"I need to come, please, baby, please..."

"Aw, that's so cute. A cop calling me baby..."

He groaned.

I rocked forward and back. For a guy who called himself straight, he had a prick that knew exactly how far to expand to hit my most sensitive places. My gland was lit up like a five-alarm fire.

Now, baby, now...

As he came, I came too, but my come was a lot more messy. It absolutely drenched his uniform shirt. Oopsy. He couldn't pass it off as spilling a cola or something. The ocean-side aroma of my spunk was the brash and unashamed scent of hard-fucking man.

"Hope you have a change of shirts in your patrol vehicle." I stepped away, smacking my lips in appreciation at the sight of his collapsed prick.

Cop, no litterbug, looked around for the small public trash-can. Since his hands were still cuffed, I took mercy on him and discarded the used rubber myself. Then I walked around the bench, still studying him.

"You look good like that, smeared with spunk, your hands cuffed out of the way, you prick hanging out of your fly. What would the chief of police think?"

I hadn't yet put my jeans back on, so Cop kept staring at my pink, twinkling ass. "He'd probably end up begging for a piece himself. How the hell do you do it to me every time? You get into my head, you fucker. I mean, you fucker, *sir*."

Like I said before, I can be merciful to a broken man, so I didn't punish him for the insolence. "Listen. While you're here. I'm opening a new dungeon, and there's going to be a party. You in?"

He laughed. "If I said no, would you believe me?"

I laughed right back.

"So why did you even ask, sir? Of course, I'm up for it. Just tell me the time and date."

PLAY

*S**tep into my dungeon, so-called straight guys. Step into the place where straight guys go gay.*

New carpet, new ceiling tiles, new plaster and paint on the walls. Underneath, hidden from view, new soundproofing made from the most advanced twenty-first century materials. The carpet and ceiling tiles were midnight black in every room except the kitchen and baths. The walls varied from room to room, depending on the theme of the individual cell in question. One room was lined with bricks, with stout metal rings set in various places in the masonry. Some rooms had dark hardwood paneling on the walls. Those rooms featured a lot of faux leather Victorian furniture, including St. Anthony's crosses and various whipping benches at various heights.

The great room was more general purpose, complete with a bar and several comfortable leather couches where people could socialize. There was an additional layer of rubber padding beneath the carpet, the better to allow subs to remain kneeling at a dom's feet for long periods of time.

The walls in every room, including the great room, were decorated not with art but with actual whips and various other pieces of equipment mounted on hooks or small shelves. Spotlights played across the most interesting pieces.

One room, off the side from the entrance hall, was lined with lockers where men could leave phones, wallets, clothes, and the rest of so-called real life behind.

We'd done well, I thought. Very damn well.

The man behind the bar wore nothing except a police-blue G-string that barely restrained his bulging package. My ex Scott. But he wasn't Scott here. He wasn't even Cop. He was just the bartender, at least for the time being. He wanted to start slow, to watch the action rather than being thrown into the middle of a full-fledged group scene, but nobody comes to one of my parties and stands around with his prick in his hands. If you don't want to fuck, you'd better be prepared to work.

As with any bar, there was a mirror behind him. The G-string let you see the blue butt-plug sticking out between his cheeks.

Bear and Wimp emerged from the changing room. As always, Bear was naked except for the magnificent growth of fur on his big body. Wimp wore his usual pink poodle collar. Bear held the leash, tugging impatiently to hurry Wimp along.

There were bowls of lube everywhere, but only a couple of boxes of rubbers. They were optional, because everybody had already passed a health test before I'd confirmed their invitation to tonight's grand opening of my new dungeon. The soundproofing meant nobody in the other units could hear what was happening in my dungeon, but people would notice the extra vehicles, so the super had already notified everyone in the building that a private party had been scheduled. Bear's neighbors didn't know the details, but they'd be made aware there was going to be a party going late, and some of them had chosen to be elsewhere for the night.

The super, of course, was one of the first people I invited to the party. In real life, he was named Stevens, but you left your real name in the locker.

Tonight, he was Rock, named for his wall of hard, smooth black muscle.

The set-up stirred my dominant blood. Men arrived in their respectable street clothes, vanished into the changing room, and then emerged as horny, hungry subjects of my total psychological control.

This party was going to be popular. So many men had submitted to me. So many so-called straight guys had already agreed to attend a gay orgy strictly on my say-so. Nobody who accepted my invitation would fail to show because they knew such failure meant they'd never get another.

Besides the bartender, Bear and Wimp, always eager, were the first to arrive. I hadn't expected anything else. They'd done most of the renovations, and now they examined their workmanship with an air of obvious pride.

"Don't look so pleased with yourself," I said. "You boys did the grunt work. I'm the genius who dreamed up the concept."

Bear stood up on his hind legs like the grizzly he was named for. His built, heavily furred body demanded the name. "I'm pretty sure you're not the first man to come up with the idea of converting a condo apartment into a private sex dungeon."

"Oho. Somebody's cruising for a bruising." I snatched a riding crop from the wall display and snapped it briskly across Bear's chest, taking aim to be sure to catch the sensitive tips of both of his flat brown nipples. His dark curls couldn't protect from the snap of my whip hand.

He whimpered.

I laughed.

Wimp swallowed a snicker, but the glint in his eyes gave him away. I smacked him across the widest part of his curvy butt. Beating his ass is always a pleasure, because his waxed body showed off every stripe.

When the front door opened and closed, we heard footsteps and voices coming down the hall and into the changing room. Poor Rock was assigned to door duty. It was a punishment detail for a punishment he hadn't earned, but hey. Somebody had to stand outside in the hall to welcome our guests, so Rock had no choice but to remain dressed in a perfectly unremarkable pair of cheap department store jeans and a baby-blue button-down shirt. Since I'd ordered my various guests to arrive at different times, the better to stagger the crowding in the parking lot and the elevator, he was going to be stuck outside for quite some time.

His dick was undoubtedly forming a huge tent in his jeans. A nice welcome for all our VIP guests.

As for me, I needed to pay attention to what was going in the great room. With a smirk, I ordered Bear onto his back, then instructed Wimp to kneel right over his face. Bear was within a tongue-stretch of being able to lick Wimp's long prick, but I refused to give him permission to take that first taste. Not just yet.

"We've got all night," I said.

"Please," Bear whined. "I need it now." His hot breath tickled the shiny skin of Wimp's long pink cock.

They both needed it now, but it pleased me to make them wait.

The newest arrivals were a couple of subs I'd played with on and off over the course of the past year. They too once claimed to be straight, but I'm pretty sure neither one of them still dated girls in their spare time.

"Help yourself." I gestured at the bar.

"Yes, sir." They turned to Cop, who poured quickly and efficiently. You'd never know he was a cop, not a real-life bartender.

I picked one guy at random to jab his prick at Wimp's face. I called him Joe, because I used to have a running gag about he was an average Joe. He had a tight, slim body that wasn't especially hairy and wasn't especially smooth. His cock was a perfectly average dick. He was just a random guy with brown hair and brown eyes, but his enthusiasm for submission made him stand out from the crowd.

"Meet Wimp, Joe," I said. "Now fuck his face."

Wimp smacked his lips happily at the hard prick he found between his lips.

The second guy was another hairy bear-type, although I didn't consider him a true bear because he was a college kid of around twenty-one or twenty-two. I called him College.

"Spread yourself over my lap, College."

"Yes, sir."

While they were at the bar, I'd swapped the riding crop for a leather paddle, all with the intention of using it on College. A paddle is more maneuverable than a crop when you've got a big hairy butt spread across your knees.

"How many times did you play with yourself this week?" I smacked his ass once on the right cheek, then on the left cheek. "I expect the truth."

"It wasn't play." College squirmed in a way that rubbed his growing prick into my upper thighs. "It was serious business, sir."

That was a request for a harder spanking if I ever heard one. I swatted his spread cheeks six or eight more times, putting more pressure into each swing. He yelped with every blow. By the fifth swat, tears were running from the corners of his eyes.

"No word games out of you today," I said. "Are we clear?"

"Yes, sir. We're clear, sir."

"You seem to think you're smart, Mr. College, but I'm smarter."

He kicked and groaned as I applied the paddle in brisk swats to his furry butt.

"Yes, sir. You're smarter, sir. Thank you, sir."

I continued to spank him— not too hard, more directing the strokes to bounce his prick into the gap between my thighs. When I had him where I wanted him, I clamped those thighs tightly closed and began to squeeze. Although we were both ridiculously hard, I had no desire to come this early in the evening. Rather, I wanted to focus on making him shame himself by coming all over my legs, belly, and prick while I spanked away on his kinky, pain-craving ass.

As he rocked up and down over my knees and under my paddled, I enjoyed my front row view of the threeway taking place on the floor at my feet. Bear was the mattress spread on his back. Since he didn't have permission to spike into Wimp's hole, he had to be content with nudging his hard prick here and there against the two bodies hunched above him. Wimp jabbed harder and harder between Bear's stretched lips, while Joe matched him stroke by stroke jabbing into Wimp's mouth.

It had been weeks for Joe, and he couldn't hold out. Grunting helplessly, he suddenly blasted deep enough to paint Wimp's

STRAIGHT TO GAY LEATHER: BUILD MY GAY DUNGEON

tonsils. That triggered Wimp to empty into Bear's mouth, which triggered me to slap unexpectedly hard on College's spread ass.

College spurted gallons of goo all over the place, including my hand, which was already tugging impatiently at my own nuts. Most of the party guests hadn't even arrived yet. No way I was letting myself come this soon.

♂♂♂

An hour later, things were getting real. I was now in the medieval dungeon, where a hidden humidifier created an atmosphere as damp and sticky as the real Middle Ages. Although the walls were gray stone, with stout iron rings set in various places around the room, the lighting was modern electric candles set in niches. They threw a flickering, near-Satanic light on the room without running the risk of throwing off any sparks. The last thing you want in a room where you've got men in chains is a fire hazard.

Nobody was getting out of my shackles quickly or easily. Nobody.

I smacked my lips in satisfaction.

A slender man, even longer and more slender because of the way his wrists were chained overhead, dangled naked from the far wall. His prick pointed straight for me. A bigger man was chained face-up on the torture bench. The chains locked around his wrists and ankles were attached to a complicated system of pulleys that were controlled by a single pull-chain. I yanked, and the pulleys creaked, a slow but sinister sound. The chains on the big man's wrist and ankles tugged more firmly, pulling his body into a more extreme spread-eagle.

I pulled again to stop the pulley. He tucked and lifted his muscular ass-cheeks from the bench, the better to thrust his prick in my direction. I tapped the pulleys on and off again, just enough to tighten his chains a skinch more. Now he shouldn't be able to move a muscle.

"Please," he begged. His pupils dilated thanks to the combination of dim light and hopeless lust. "Please, just fucking please." Thick streams of pre-cum ran down his shaft, the gooey liquid catching the flickering flame of the electric candles.

The only man not yet chained was on all fours on the stone floor. Utterly still, afraid to breathe, he seemed to believe he could escape my notice if only he remained quiet enough.

Fat chance of that. I smacked at the widest part of his exposed ass cheeks with my riding crop.

"Stand."

"Yes, sir." He stumbled a little, the way you do when you've been holding yourself frozen for far too long. His prick threw off several hot drops of pre-fuck sauce.

"Lick that up."

He dropped back down the stone floor with his tongue thrust out. Three swipes of his pink tongue, and the job was done.

"I said stand."

"Yes, sir."

"Get on that fucking bench."

He didn't comment on the fact that a very large man was already chained to the bench in question. My party guests knew better than to quibble about things like that. As he climbed awkwardly on top of the prisoner on the bench, the big man's erect prick jabbed here and there— against his toned belly, between his thighs, finally positioning itself so it was dangerously close to shoving itself into the smaller man's pink hole.

STRAIGHT TO GAY LEATHER: BUILD MY GAY DUNGEON

"There's a lot of so-called straight guys at this party tonight for some reason," I said. "You happen to be one of them?"

The smaller guy shifted uneasily on top of the chained man. He wasn't sure what I wanted to hear.

I slapped Small's naked shoulders with the riding crop. "Answer me."

"Yes, sir."

"Explain the attraction of this kind of party to a straight man."

"I, um, I'm a submissive, sir. It isn't really submission if I'm being ordered to do something I'd do in my ordinary life. Sir. Like, if a woman orders me to fuck her, that doesn't seem too submissive. It just seems... I don't know. Kind of lame?"

That made sense, especially since it was a tale I'd heard from other guys like him.

"You read your paperwork when you underwent the health exam, correct? Don't tell me what you think I want to hear. Tell me the truth."

"Yes, sir. I did read the paperwork."

"You agreed to submit to whatever I order you to do. That's the price of attending one of my parties."

"Yes, sir." Small wriggled uneasily. The chained man underneath him adjusted himself to make sure his peckerhead continued to press against his squirming hole.

"But you have an objection."

"No, sir."

I slashed out with the whip. Shoulders, butt, thigh. "Tell the truth."

"You should chain me, sir. Force me to ride him."

"You know why I'm not chaining you?"

Even in the flicker of the faux candlelight, his face flushed red. "Yes, sir."

"Tell me. Say it. Everybody in this dungeon wants to hear you say it."

"It's more shameful if I fuck him of my free own will, sir."

"That's right. You can't deny you wanted his prick up your ass. I'm tired of hearing your denials. Sit down, and start riding." I smacked harder with the riding crop, and Small's curved ass began its long, slow slide down the chained man's fat shaft.

The guy hanging from the wall rattled his chains to attract my attention. His shaft poked halfway across the room.

We all ignored him. The focus was on the chained man spread-eagled on the torture bench, his body so stretched it was painful for him to lift and thrust. Yet he couldn't resist lifting and thrusting to go deeper, ever deeper into Small's grasping rectum. It was a delicious paradox. If Chains wanted the pleasure, he had to accept the pain.

"Ride him, Small," I said. "I want to see you gallop. Faster! Faster!" I underlined every word with a stroke from the riding crop.

Small knew how to move his ass. Despite the whip slashing at his backside, he cried out in pure pleasure when he sat so hard on Chains's upthrust shaft that Small's tunnel completely swallowed it out of sight. His hairy balls bounced, but I could see only a hint of root. It was a true balls-deep fuck.

My own clothes were long gone. All I wore at the moment was a medieval-style steel chain around my neck with several stout iron keys serving as pendants. They rattled against my chest as I went back to the pulley, adjusting it to allow Chains on the bench a little more freedom of movement. His arms and legs still fought the cuffs, but his ass could lift higher off the bench to propel his hard prick deeper and deeper into Small's welcoming butthole.

"Please." The naked guy hanging off the wall was frantic by now. "I'll do anything."

"I know you will," I said. "I've always known that. You're the only one who didn't accept that."

"Please, sir. Just give me the chance."

There's nothing was slick or noiseless in a medieval dungeon. When I inserted the key in the iron cuffs, the lock creaked in protest, as if it didn't want to open.

Hanging Man groaned. His muscles went even more tense than they were before, if that's even possible. He was bracing himself.

I worked the lock harder. The cuffs creaked, then finally popped open. Hanging Man's arms must be pins-and-needles, but he brought them down fast to break his fall onto a floor that looked like stone but was actually made of that same bouncy stuff you find in children's parks. In another life, he'd studied gymnastics, and he knew how to fall. Rolling lightly onto his back, he looked up at me with an expression of raw hunger in his eyes.

"I'm so grateful you set me free, sir," he said.

"Who said you're free?" I tapped the tip of the riding crop at a random on the floor. "Kneel."

"Yes, sir!"

He obeyed with alacrity. Just another straight guy who hungered to be humiliated by a gay man with a superior grasp of human psychology.

"Suck it." I braced my feet far apart on the floor, the better to stick my hard-on at him at the level of his lips.

"Yes, sir."

On the bench, Small was still slow-fucking Chains. They must both be rubbed raw, and there was little chance they'd be spurting again anytime soon, but they remained interlocked, with the unchained man's semi doing its dance inside the chained man, whose own semi was trapped between their writhing bellies.

The lips locked around my peckerhead gobbled me slowly, sensuously. Hanging Man had spent a lot of time hanging on that cold stone wall, and he'd like the cocksucking portion of the evening to last just as long. Too bad, so sad, because I had a lot of other subs and slaves to attend to.

"That's enough," I said.

Anxious to prove how obedient he was, anxious to avoid another session hanging in chains, he spat me out immediately. Sitting back on his haunches, he let me see the panic in his eyes.

"Speak."

"Please, sir. I can do better. I can do more."

"You did fine. You've been practicing, haven't you?"

He flushed. "Yes, sir."

"Excellent. But now I need something else. Get on all-fours."

When he obeyed, his ass lifted beautifully to my riding crop. I enjoyed smacking him time and again to create a pattern of flushed stripes on his taut flesh. He'd developed some technique for clapping his ass-cheeks open, a dangerous technique to show off, because it tempted me to spank into his crack.

"Ouch!" But there was victory, as well as pain, his voice.

STRAIGHT TO GAY LEATHER: BUILD MY GAY DUNGEON

The guys on the bench had completely recovered their stiffies. Although the wheels weren't turning, the pulleys, the chains, and the hard iron legs made rattle sounds as the two men bounced together and apart and together again.

The ass in front of me clapped open wider, showing me the pink of his flushed, hairless hole.

"Stand." There were hours of party left, and I was in no hurry to grab a fast four-on-the-floor fuck.

Hanging Man stood.

"Face the wall. Hands braced on the wall at about shoulder height."

He obeyed. It was a position that let him lean into the stone while pushing his ass back to welcome me inside his squirming tunnel.

"Tell me what's going to happen to you."

"You're going to fuck me, sir."

"I need more."

"You're going to fuck me. Up the ass. While..." He shrugged his bare shoulders in the direction of the torture bench. "While those guys are watching."

"That's right, straight guy. You're getting fucked. And everybody's going to know it. Not just these guys. Everybody out there. Everybody at this whole damn party."

He whimpered.

"Don't cry."

"I'm not crying, sir."

"How many people you think I invited to this party?"

He whimpered louder. "I don't know, sir. A lot, sir!"

I snorted and thrust forward. His pink asshole didn't offer the slightest resistance. I don't know what kind of sex toy he'd been practicing with, but it was large. I could stroke into him balls-deep without catching my breath, and that's exactly what I did.

I've been so good. I've been orchestrating all the action at this party, and I've kept myself from spewing.

"Don't deny yourself, sir. Please don't deny yourself on my account." Hanging Man must be reading my thoughts.

"You want me to come deep in your ass, don't you? Say it."

"Yes, sir. Spunk my ass, sir." His talented interior rippled all around my first shaft.

Why hold back? I came a gusher at the exact same moment the two men on the torture bench spurted another load.

♂♂♂

The dungeon was now in full swing. I spent an indefinite amount of time going from cell to cell, barking out orders, often slashing out with my choice of whips or paddle. Everywhere I went, men were being fucked in the face or the butt. Everywhere, striped asses were trembling between greedy tongues, probing fingers, and thrusting pricks.

As the evening went on, more and more toys came into play. "Plug that butt," I'd command, and somebody would insert a fat unyielding plug into another man's quivering hole.

"He needs the buzztoy," I'd say, and a receptive ass would find itself filled with a remote control vibrator.

One guy was spread-eagled face-down on a bed, arms and legs cuffed to the four bedposts, a long pair of anal beads mostly buried between his ass-cheeks. I tugged the string just enough to pull out a single bead.

"More, sir. Please, more! If you pull it out fast, I'll come."

I swatted his ass with the nearest slapper. "You're not coming yet. I like watching you sweat."

"Please, sir."

"Keep begging. I like to hear you beg."

There were thirty-seven people at this party, enough to keep all the cells filled and still have some people hanging out in the great room. I returned to the bar, walking past multiple groups of naked men wet with spunk and sweat, most of them covered in red bruises or pink stripes.

Only the bartender remained untouched. He stood there, his ignored cock stuck out for miles in front of him, a pleading expression on his face, as he mixed me a pink martini. Was I even going to drink it, or did I just enjoy frustrating him?

He shook it several times in a silver shaker and strained it into a double-sized martini glass with a pink sugar rim. The final touch was a pink cherry.

I crinkled my eyebrows together. Took a cautious sip.

"Please, sir," he said. "Please." His gaze swept the room behind me, so achingly full of men collapsed on leather pillows to sleep off the nastiest group scene of their lives. "I've been very good."

I set down my glass. "I suppose you have. Yet it's my perfect right to punish you anyway. This is a dungeon. Your ideas of right and wrong don't matter here."

"Please, sir. Dear fuck, please!"

"Come around the counter. Crawl on your belly."

"Sir, I'm too hard, sir! How can I crawl when I'm this fucking hard?"

"My way or no way."

He dropped to all fours, but I shook my head. When I say crawl, I mean it.

Groaning, he dropped all the way down on his belly to inchworm across the floor. A whipping would have been more pleasant than the way his hard-on was getting ground into the dirt, but he didn't need my mercy. He needed my harshness.

It seemed to take hours for him to make his way out from behind the bars, although it couldn't have been more than a couple of minutes. He didn't dare to whimper, but tears glistened at the corners of his eyes.

"Lick my toes."

He lifted his face to the place where my long feet were hooked around the lower rung of the bar stool. Panting, snuffling, he thrust out his tongue to probe between the sensitive webbing of my prehensile toes. My feet were undoubtedly sweaty, but he'd never been afraid of a little sweat.

"Mmmm." He hummed into my feet, the better to let me feel those oral vibrations. His way of telling me how good his mouth would feel once it was wrapped around my prick. A hint.

But I didn't take hints. Immediately discarding any plan to grant him permission to suck my shaft, I pointed for the only remaining empty piece of furniture— a black leather ottoman. "Drape yourself over that. Ass up."

He hurried to obey. The small, firm square forced him to pose on his hands and knees, all the better to press his prick hard into the leather.

It was too late in the night for him to require much warm-up. The party had been going on too long, and he'd had a front-row view for much of the dirty doings. I fingered him a moment, then opened him with the head of my prick by stroking between his cheeks and against his hole a couple of times before thrusting the entirety of my shaft deep inside. His flexible tunnel spread eagerly for me, sending a jolt of power straight to my brain.

I'd come several times already tonight, but I'd come again, even if it was a dry come. His grasping ass would guarantee it.

"Who built this dungeon?" I asked as I hammered in and out.

"We did, sir."

"Who owns this dungeon?"

"You do, sir."

"Fuck, yes. And don't even of you squirming worms ever fucking forget it." It felt good, but my previous releases meant I didn't experience the same urgency as I had earlier in the evening. I could take my time, dick around, stop and smell the roses. "Hey." When I raised my voice, everybody in the room snapped to attention. "Everybody with a hard-on, get your horny ass over here. Make a circle around us."

Many of the guys were spunked out, but at least eight panting horndogs hurried to form the circle. It was almost too many guys. Me and Cop were completely surrounded by naked, hairy, muscular male legs. Hands hovered, but nobody dared to touch himself until I gave the order.

"Time yourselves carefully," I said. "I want to feel a rain of spunk when I give the command, and not one minute earlier. Somebody bring on the lube."

Guys too sore to fondle themselves formed a second ring around the ring of eight, the better to pass around tubes of lube or cold drinks— and, of course, also to shove in for a view of the action they could get between all those big, broad shoulders.

Tears were streaming down Cop's face. He was no longer on all fours. Instead, he was balanced on his chin, his left hand, and his knees. His right hand kept tugging at his own nuts, the better to delay his moment. Poor guy. He was the only one who hadn't already come multiple times, and he was frantic that he'd come before I did.

"That's good," I said. "That's a good boy. Pace yourself. Ooh, that tight straight-boy ass feels so good around my cock."

My own balls throbbed. There couldn't be any fluid left, but I was still going to reverberate.

"Now," I screamed. "Now. All of you... blast right fucking now!"

We exploded together. Maybe it was male hormones spurring us on, that ancient competitive instinct that's so natural between men, but we were all coming in hot spurty gushers of a size and strength I'd never expected. Yes, I'd known Cop would spew out a lake on the floor, but I had no idea I'd somehow come out with another quart of fluid. Nor did I realize the eight men around me would literally rain down a thundershower on my naked back. It was the biggest, sloppiest, ten-way hose-off I'd ever experienced.

Best party ever. And that was only Night One of my new dungeon.

♂♂♂

Other Books by This Author

*Straight to Gay Hookups: The Complete No Strings Attached

To stay free and easy, a college student decides to start hooking up with straight guys. It's amazing how many men in his town are eager to meet him in secret. And then the threeways begin...

*Straight to Gay College: The Tutor Goes Wild

Before this tutor has finished giving lessons, former straight guys have gained a complete education including advanced topics like double penetration and group games— everything they'll need to know to get an A from their kinky professor.

*Straight to Gay Confessions: First Time Trilogy

Three red-hot stories about a college student's journey from lonely straight guy to hard-partying gay.

About the Author

Bro Biggly interviews men about sex and then writes about it. Nice work if you can get it.

Follow Bro on Amazon[1] to keep up with his latest releases.

---

1. https://www.amazon.com/Bro-Biggly/e/B079YKTDJH

Made in the USA
Columbia, SC
23 November 2024